Uncle Grubby

This story shows the value of patience.
What takes a little time can be well worth the wait.

Story by:
Will Ryan

Illustrated by:
David High
Russell Hicks
Doug McCarthy
Theresa Mazurek
Allyn Conley/Gorniak
Julie Armstrong

WORLDS OF WONDER™

Grubby®   Newton Gimmick™   Princess Aruzia™   Leota™   Wooly What's-It™

Prince Arin™   Fobs®

Fobs are happy creatures that come in a rainbow of colors.

There in a clearing were three little Fob eggs.

Out of the orange, purple and blue eggs popped three baby Fobs!

We said good-bye to Frank and Fay Fob and their new baby Fobs.